JANE SEYMOUR · JAMES KEACH

THIS ONE 'N THAT ONE

in

And Then There Were
Three!
......a new arrival

illustrated by Geoffrey Planer

ANGEL GATE

Los Angeles

Angel Gate, a division of Left Field Ink, Inc.
3111 W. Burbank Blvd., Suite 103, Burbank, CA 91505
Printed in China.
Designed by Claire Moore. Text set in Gill Sans.
Library of Congress Cataloging-in-publication Data
Seymour, Jane. /And Then There Were Three
Jane Seymour and James Keach; illustrated by Geoffrey Planer.
p. cm. (This One and That One)
Summary: The kittens are pleased when they find Mom is pregnant but
bringing up a baby is not quite what they imagined.
[1. Cats-Fiction. 2. Parents and child-Fiction. 3. Pregnant-Fiction.]
I. Keach, James. II. Planer, Geoffrey, ill. III. Title IV.
Series PZ7.S5235Tj 1998
[E] – dc21 98-4788 CIP AC
Library of Congress Control Number: 2003093064
ISBN 1-932431-09-8
First Impression

To
Kris and John
Kalen, Katie, Jenni, Sean, Thea, Erica,
Nina, Tom and Fizzy,
our inspirational friend Christopher Reeve, and
Jan of course!
And all the kids and kits around the world!

Something funny was going on!
THIS ONE and **THAT ONE** were sure of i
Mom was whispering to Dad.

Dad was whispering to Granny.

Mom was phoning Auntie ....
.... and everyone was looking
like there was some big secret.

THIS ONE and **THAT ONE** played at being spies.

They hid behind the sofa when Mom and Dad were talking.

"How are you feeling, Mom?" asked Dad.

"Really big," said Lady Jane.

"Bigger?" chuckled Big Jim.

"Biggest!" laughed Lady Jane.

"Maybe we should tell the little ones now?" she said.

"Maybe we should - let's go and find them," said Big Jim.

Down behind the sofa **THIS ONE** looked at **THAT ONE**.
THAT ONE looked at **THIS ONE**.
"Mom's getting bigger and bigger!" said **THIS ONE**.
".... and she's going to pop her buttons!" said **THAT ONE**.
"That can only mean one thing!" said **THIS ONE**.
"Yup!" said **THAT ONE**.

Then Big Jim and Lady Jane came back into the room.

They were surprised to see the kittens there.

"We were looking for you! Dad and I have something impor-
tant to tell you," said Mom, with a little smile.

"We know already!" said **THIS ONE**.

"We sure do!" said **THAT ONE**!

"Oh?" said Mom.

"So?" said Dad.

"You've got to eat less ...." said **THIS ONE**.

"Well - wipe my whiskers!"
chuckled Dad as he
rubbed his nose.

"Well - tug my tail!"
giggled Mom and
she wiped her eyes.

"Oh my dear kittens - no I do not need to go on a diet! But I am getting bigger - because we are going to have another kitten!"

THIS ONE looked at **THAT ONE**.
THAT ONE looked at **THIS ONE**.
"Why do we need another kitten?"
asked **THAT ONE**.

"Where are we going to get it
from?" asked **THIS ONE**.

"I'm going to have it! My kitten!
Our kitten! It's growing in my
tummy!" said Mom.

"You mean we're going to have a little brother?"
said **THIS ONE**.
".... or a little sister," said Dad.

THIS ONE and **THAT ONE** were very quiet that day.

THIS ONE and **THAT ONE** were very quiet that evening.

THIS ONE and **THAT ONE** were very quiet that night.

But when they woke up next morning they were extremely noisy.

"I'm going to take him to the beach!"
shouted **THIS ONE** as he ran round the bedroom.

"We're going to dig to China!"
said **THAT ONE** as he jumped on his bed.

"He's going to be my best friend!" said **THIS ONE**.

"No he's going to be MY best friend!" said **THAT ONE**.

"No mine!" said **THIS ONE**.

"NO MINE!" said **THAT ONE**; and they would have started to fight if Mom hadn't come in.

"**THE OTHER ONE** is going to be OUR best friend," she said - and she gave them both a kiss.

As the weeks passed Lady Jane's tummy
got bigger and bigger.
When she sat down for a rest
she let the kittens feel it.

Sometimes they thought they could
feel someone moving inside.

One bright morning **THIS ONE** and **THAT ONE** bounced into the kitchen for breakfast - but Mom and Dad were not there. Instead Granny Purrfect sat alone at the table.

"You two are going to have to be extra good and play by yourselves today. Mom has gone to the hospital to have the new kitten!" she purred.

THIS ONE and **THAT ONE** were really excited when
Mom and Dad came home next day.
They ran down the path to meet them.

Mom carried a little bundle in her arms and
after she'd kissed them she bent down
carefully so the kittens could peek in.

"What tiny paws!"
said **THIS ONE** surprised.

"What a squashy face!"
said **THAT ONE** amazed.

"What shall we call her?" asked Mom.

"HER?!" said **THIS ONE**.

"A GIRL?!" said **THAT ONE**.

"NOT A BOY?" said **THIS ONE** and **THAT ONE** together.

"A girl," said Mom.

"A sister," said Dad.

"Oh!" said **THIS ONE** and **THAT ONE** together.

"What shall we call her?" asked Big Jim.
"We'll call her **THE OTHER ONE**,"
said **THIS ONE** and **THAT ONE** together.

"**THE OTHER ONE** it is!" laughed Lady Jane.

"I'll need your help boys, I'm really tired and **THE OTHER ONE** will need a lot of looking after," explained Lady Jane later on.

"You can watch after her when I've fed her," said Mom, ".... and rock her; and rub her back; and play with her; and wipe her nose; and change her diapers; and mop her up; and get her dressed!"

"Dresses?"
said **THIS ONE**.
"Oh!"
said **THAT ONE**.

"Icky?" said **THIS ONE**.   "Nasty!" said **THAT ONE**.

"Noisy?!"
said **THIS ONE**.

"Slimey!" said **THAT ONE** .

"Diapers?" said **THIS ONE** .

"Poooo!" said **THAT ONE** .

"Stinky!" said **THIS ONE** .

"Yucky!" said **THAT ONE** .

"We're not sure we like little kittens!"
said **THIS ONE** and **THAT ONE** together.
Big Jim and Lady Jane laughed.
"She's just like you were when you were little.
She's a purrfect little kitten!"

And they looked over at the **THE OTHER ONE** cuddled
in Mom's arms. **THE OTHER ONE** blew a bubble,
gave a gurgle and a big hiccup and looked back
at them with a twinkle in her eye.

"She sees me!" said **THIS ONE**.
"I like her!" said **THAT ONE**.
"I love her!" said **THIS ONE**.

"She's my new friend!" said **THAT ONE**.

"She's my best friend!" said **THIS ONE**.

"No she's my best new friend!" said **THAT ONE**.

"No she's my........" said **THIS ONE**,

but Lady Jane and Big Jim gave them both a hug.

"**THE OTHER ONE** is our new best friend!" laughed Lady Jane.